P9-DFN-987

NOV - - 2006

To Arden and Alisa: keep dancing — JW

Thanks to Pierre Brueghel — MF

Text copyright © 2008 Jan Wahl

Illustrations copyright © 2008 Monique Felix

Published in 2008 by Creative Editions

P.O. Box 227, Mankato, MN 56002 USA

Creative Editions is an imprint of The Creative Company.

Designed by Rita Marshall

All rights reserved. No part of the contents of this book may be reproduced

by any means without the written permission of the publisher.

Printed in Italy

Library of Congress Cataloging-in-Publication Data

Wahl, Jan.

Bear dance / by Jan Wahl; illustrated by Monique Felix.

Summary: A wild bear escapes capture and returns to his beloved

home in the mountains, where he enjoys dancing to the sounds of nature.

ISBN 978-1-56846-199-1

1. Bears—Juvenile fiction. [1. Bears—Fiction. 2. Dance—Fiction.]

I. Félix, Monique, ill. II. Title.

PZ10.3.W1295Be 2008

[E]—dc22   2007027021

First edition

2 4 6 8 9 7 5 3 1

JAN WAHL & MONIQUE FELIX

BEAR DANCE

CREATIVE EDITIONS

MANKATO, MINNESOTA

Bear stood in the middle

of the very green forest.

He began to dance.

He danced to soft rustle

of leaves in the trees.

He danced to bluebirds' sweet

feathery music.

He closed his eyes, and danced

on wildflowers in the wild

blowing wind.

He danced until the moon rose

and moonrays tickled his feet.

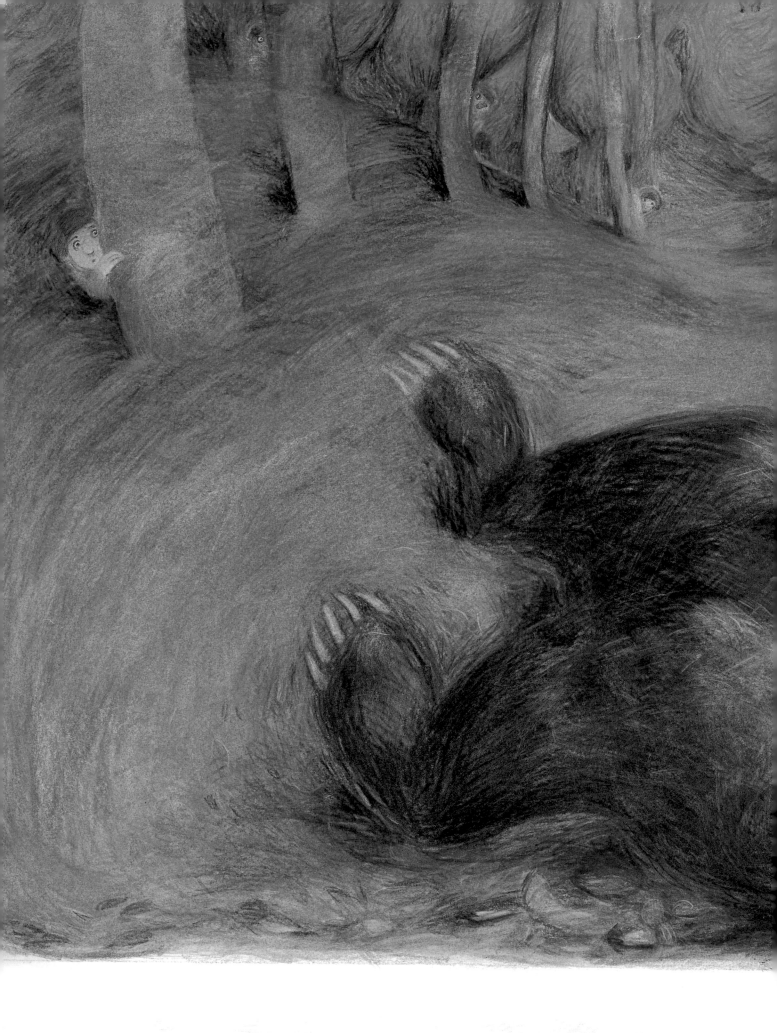

Then Bear lay on the cool grass

and slept in his warm fur.

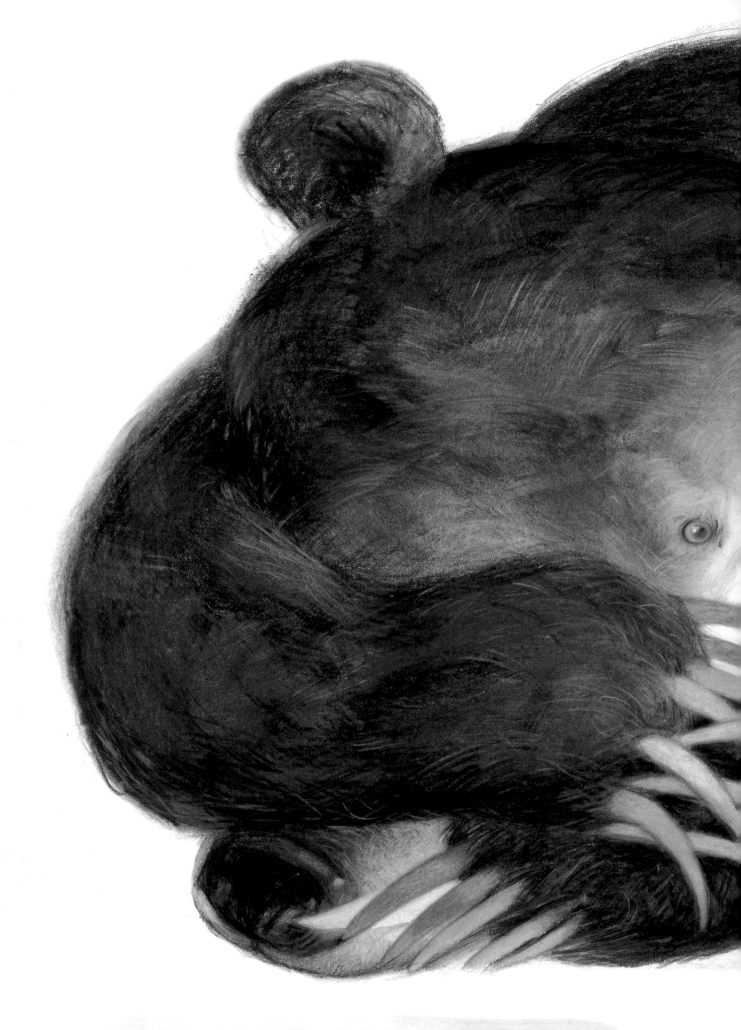

Suddenly he awoke. Men wearing

red hats pushed him into a cage.

His ears and feet spilled out through

the bars as they carried him away.

For days he had nothing to eat,

no nuts or berries.

Then they fed him his favorite things

if he stood on his hind legs.

Someone played a violin;

someone beat a drum.

They gave him pieces of honeycomb

if he swayed and hopped

to the beat of the drum.

They tied bells on him,

and led him with a rope

to the marketplace.

"DANCE, BEAR, DANCE!"

they shouted.

Slowly he danced;

the drum beat faster.

A crowd clapped hands as Bear

hopped to the violin's sharp shrill tune.

He danced until his feet hurt;

he wished he might dip them

into the soothing water of a

remembered stream.

The men in red hats built a fire

and talked late into the night.

Bear closed his ears to the

noisy laughter.

But Bear had clever paws.

With care, bit by bit,

 he pulled off the chain

 and loosened the bells.

And he crept away.

Then he ran in the bright

 starry night through fields

of mustard and clover.

And climbed over rocks higher and higher—

to the peak of a purple mountain.

There he licked tender paws,
washing them in patches of snow.

He took a sleepy nap
in the afternoon's yellow sun.

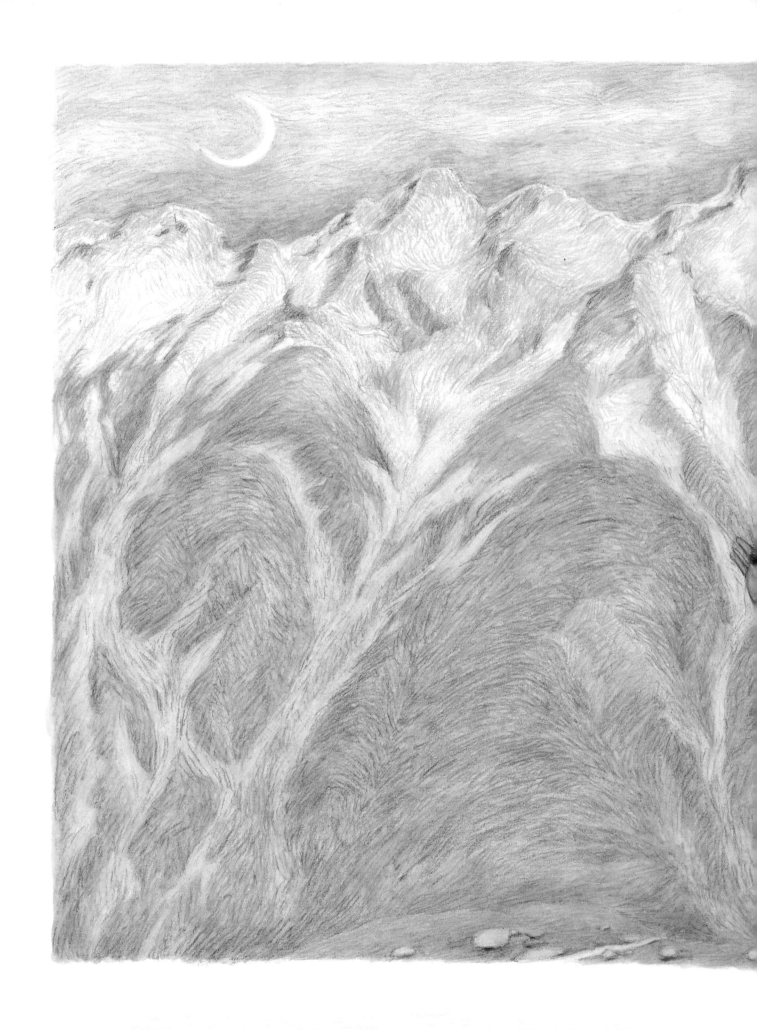

Then Bear rose to his full furry height

and he danced and he danced!